Franklin and the Scooter

From an episode of the animated TV series *Franklin,*
produced by Nelvana Limited, Neurones France s.a.r.l. and
Neurones Luxembourg S.A., based on the Franklin books
by Paulette Bourgeois and Brenda Clark.

Story written by Sharon Jennings.

Illustrated by Céleste Gagnon, Sasha McIntyre, Violeta Nikolic
and Jelena Sisic.

Based on the TV episode *Franklin and the Red Scooter,*
written by Bob Ardiel.

TM Kids Can Read is a trademark of Kids Can Press Ltd.

Franklin

Franklin is a trademark of Kids Can Press Ltd.
The character of Franklin was created by Paulette Bourgeois and Brenda Clark.
Text © 2004 Contextx Inc.
Illustrations © 2004 Brenda Clark Illustrator Inc.

Kids Can Press acknowledges the financial support of the Government of Ontario,
through the Ontario Media Development Corporation's Ontario Book Initiative;
the Ontario Arts Council; the Canada Council for the Arts; and the Government
of Canada, through the BPIDP, for our publishing activity.

Published in Canada by
Kids Can Press Ltd.
29 Birch Avenue
Toronto, ON M4V 1E2

Published in the U.S. by
Kids Can Press Ltd.
2250 Military Road
Tonawanda, NY 14150

www.kidscanpress.com

Series editor: Tara Walker
Edited by Jennifer Stokes
Designed by Céleste Gagnon

Printed in Hong Kong, China, by Wing King Tong

The hardcover edition of this book is smyth sewn casebound.
The paperback edition of this book is limp sewn with a drawn-on cover.

CM 04 0 9 8 7 6 5 4 3 2 1
CM PA 04 0 9 8 7 6 5 4 3 2 1

National Library of Canada Cataloguing in Publication Data

Jennings, Sharon
        Franklin and the scooter / Sharon Jennings ; illustrated by Violeta
Nikolic, Sasha McIntyre, Céleste Gagnon, Jelena Sisic.

(Kids Can read)
The character Franklin was created by Paulette Bourgeois and Brenda Clark.
ISBN 1-55337-493-2 (bound).   ISBN 1-55337-494-0 (pbk.)

I. Nikolic, Violeta II. McIntyre, Sasha III. Jelena Sisic IV. Céleste Gagnon
V. Bourgeois, Paulette VI. Clark, Brenda VII. Title. VIII. Series: Kids Can read
(Toronto, Ont.)

PS8569.E563F7174 2004   jC813'.54   C2003-904251-0

Kids Can Press is a /©r\S™ Entertainment company

SUGAR GROVE PUBLIC LIBRARY DISTRICT
54 Snow Street/P.O. Box 1049
Sugar Grove, IL 60554
(630) 466-4686

Damage noted Date 8/0/23 Staff Initial RO

Markings/Writing_____ Water/Liquid ✓_____

Loose/Weak Binding_____ Stains_____
Other_ pages curled from moisture._

Pages/Location_____

Franklin and the Scooter

Kids Can Press

Franklin can tie his shoes.

Franklin can count by twos.

And Franklin can ride

a bicycle and a scooter, too.

There is only one problem.

Franklin doesn't have a scooter.

Franklin's friend Rabbit has a scooter.

One day, Rabbit let Franklin ride it.

It was shiny and red

and went really, really fast.

"This is fun!" said Franklin.

"I want my own scooter."

Franklin went home.

"I want a scooter," he said.

"May I have one for my birthday?"

"You just had your birthday,"

said his mother.

"You got lots of nice things,"

said his father.

Franklin had an idea.

"You may take back

some of those things," he said.

"Then you can buy me a scooter."

His parents laughed.

"Maybe next year," said his mother.

That afternoon, Franklin and Bear
walked to the store.

"Are you getting a scooter?" Bear asked.

"No," said Franklin.

"My dad said a scooter costs
too much money."

"Oh," said Bear.

Franklin and Bear looked in the window.

They stared at all the shiny, new scooters.

Then Bear had
an idea.

"Why don't *you* buy a scooter?"
asked Bear. "You have lots of money
in your piggybank."

Franklin smiled.
"Yes, I do!" he said.

He and Bear ran back to Franklin's house.

Franklin shook out
his piggybank.

He counted all the pennies,
nickels, dimes and quarters.

"This is not a lot of money,"

said Franklin.

"It is just enough to buy

two ice cream cones," said Bear.

The next day, Franklin had a good idea.

"I will sell lemonade," he said.

Bear came over to help.

They mixed sugar
and water.

They squeezed lemons.

They set up a table in front of the house.

They tasted the lemonade lots of times.

It was just right.

Then they saw Beaver.

"Want to buy some lemonade?"

Franklin asked. "You look very hot."

"I am very hot," said Beaver.

"I just had a turn on Rabbit's scooter."

"I'm getting my own scooter, soon,"

said Franklin.

Beaver gave Franklin her money.

Franklin picked up

the lemonade.

The jug was empty.

"Oops," said Bear.

Franklin gave back the money.

The next day, Franklin had another idea.

"I will sell some of my toys," he said.

Franklin looked in his toy box.

He found lots of toys.

But then he changed his mind.

"I *love* my toys," he told his mother.

"Maybe I can sell some of *your* toys."

Franklin's mother gave him old books and old clothes.

His father gave him an old chair and an old lamp.

His sister gave him an old doll.

"Now I have lots to sell!" said Franklin.

But nobody wanted to buy.

"Who wants old stuff?" asked Beaver.

"Are you
selling food?"
asked Bear.

Then Rabbit came by on his scooter.

He saw Franklin's bicycle.

"Can I buy your bike?" he asked.

"It isn't for sale," said Franklin.

"I really want a bicycle," said Rabbit.

"But my parents won't buy me one."

"Hmmm," said Franklin.

Franklin jumped up.

"I have a good idea!" he said.

"If I sell you my bicycle,

I'll have lots of money to buy a scooter!"

"Good idea!" said Rabbit.

He held up his piggybank.

"I have lots of money!"

Rabbit shook out pennies,

nickels, dimes and quarters.

Everyone counted the coins.

"This is not a lot of money,"

said Franklin.

"This is just enough to buy

two ice cream cones,"

said Bear.

Rabbit was sad.

"I really, *really* want a bicycle," he said.

Franklin was sad.

"I really, really, *really* want a scooter," he said.

"Hmmm," said Rabbit.

"Hmmm," said Franklin.

Then Franklin and Rabbit jumped up.

"I HAVE A GOOD IDEA!!"

they shouted together.

"We will switch back and forth

every day!" said Franklin.

"We will take turns sharing!" said Rabbit.

Franklin rode off

on Rabbit's scooter.

Rabbit rode off

on Franklin's bicycle.

Beaver and Bear ran after them.

They all met at the ice cream store.

They had just enough money

to buy four ice cream cones!